GNIT-WIT GNIPPER
AND THE
DEVIOUS DRAGON

Episode Three
of
The Misadventures of Gnipper the Gnome

WRITTEN BY
T.J. LANTZ

ILLUSTRATED BY
ANA SANTO

This book is a **ROSEHAVEN** adventure.
What exactly is Rosehaven?

Rosehaven is a multi-series Fantasy world, in which mythological creatures live in hiding on the outskirts of Human exploration. It currently consists of three separate book series: Rosehaven, The Misadventure of Gnipper the Gnome, and The Dudley Diaries. Each of these series contains overlapping setting and characters, but differ in tone and reading level. The goal of Rosehaven is to offer young children an enjoyable fantasy world that grows with them as they become stronger readers. Currently Rosehaven offers:

The Misadventure of Gnipper the Gnome (For ages 7 and up, fully illustrated single sitting reads of about 50 pages. The order they are read does not matter.):

This series tells the story of Gnipper Tallhat, a twelve year old Gnome desperately trying to earn respect in her community for her scientific inventions. Unfortunately, everything she does seems to backfire.

Gnit-Wit Gnipper and the Perilous Plague
Gnit-Wit Gnipper and the Ferocious Fire-Ants
Gnit-Wit Gnipper and the Devious Dragon

The Dudley Diaries (For ages 9 and up, fully illustrated single sitting reads of about 50 pages. The order they are read does not matter):

Follows the tales of Sir Dudley Tinklebutton, a knight of the Coalition of the Burning Heart. Sir Dudley isn't your typical heroic knight: he's scared of insects, he's never slain anything, and he's only chivalrous when he thinks he can get something out of it. Can Sir Dudley overcome his cowardly qualities to become the hero he needs to be?

Sir Dudley Tinklebutton and the Dragon's Lair
Sir Dudley Tinklebutton and the Sword of Cowardice
Sir Dudley Tinklebutton and the Unholy Grail

Rosehaven (For ages 10 and up. Novels, 300+ pages, intended to be read in order):

This tells the main story of the *retics*, creatures forced into hiding by a group of Humans tasked with hunting them down. It follows the lives of several key figures: Jaxon the loud-mouthed demon who can control the elements, Tyranna the shape-shifter, learning to come to grips with her new world, and Reginald, a thousand year old Tree-ent knight dedicated to saving as many lives as he can. Together they must navigate conflicts in the Human world, and in their own community, before war wipes the retics out forever.

Rise of the Retics (Book 1)
Return of the Fae-blood (Book 2)

"Gnanny's been robbed!" yelped Gnipper. The empty room was vastly different than usual—no wall full of cuckoo clocks chiming every three minutes, no framed finger-painted wall tapestries, no statue of a centaur riding a unicycle. There was nothing left except boring walls and a dust covered floor. Even the annoying meow of Canvas, Gnanny's grumpy tail-less cat was missing. Gnipper shivered at the eerie silence.

"Step back, Gnip. The thieves may still be here and they could be dangerous."

Gnipper stepped aside as Sam, her best friend and Rosehaven's top pre-teen swords-squirrel, drew her silver, basket-handled blades and surveyed the room. Her bushy black tail puffed out, making her look larger than usual.

"Clear," she announced after a few moments. "I'll check upstairs. Don't move from that spot. Understand?"

The Gnome nodded vigorously, stopping only when one of her pink ponytails awkwardly flew into her mouth. Sam was using her don't-you-dare-question-me voice, which Gnipper never dared to question.

As Sam bounded up the stairs, Gnipper strained to listen for sounds from the second floor. Sam wouldn't even squeak a floorboard—she never did. She was respected among the Squirrel-kin for being acrobatic and light on her feet, a great honor within a species known for those attributes.

"AAAAAAAAHHHHHHH." The scream broke through the silence like flatulence in a library. It was Gnanny's voice! She was in trouble.

"I'm coming Gnanny," squealed Gnipper. She ran up the stairs, totally ignoring Sam's commands, but tripping only two times before she reached the top.

"Gnanny, I'll save you!" She screamed in her most intimidating voice (which, unfortunately for her, wouldn't have scared a ladybug).

"Save me from what, dear?" Gnanny Gnogglebottom answered as she tried to catch her breath. "Oh, that little yelp. Sam just startled me is all. I'm fine though, I swear. I will tell you though, you could give an old Gnome a heart attack sneaking up on me like that Ms. Bushytail. I know your father taught you better. How is Alastar anyway? Is he seeing anyone?"

"Gnanny," said Sam. "Don't you think a more appropriate topic of conversation, outside of my father's courting intentions, would be to explain about the robbery?"

"Robbery? Who was robbed? Certainly not me. No one on this entire island would dare touch my belongings. I have a reputation for being quite a tough one, you know."

"Of course, Gnanny," said Gnipper. "But if your stuff wasn't stolen, then where is it?"

"Well, I sold it of course. I needed the Dragon-marks for a *great* investment opportunity."

"You sold everything you have?" asked Gnipper. "Why would you ever do that? You love your stuff!"

"That's a bit of a long story. Why don't you two sit down? I don't have any chairs left, but the floor is clean. Well, it will be once I buy a new broom."

"It's alright, Gnanny," Gnipper answered. "We'll stand. Sam doesn't like to sit anyway. She says it makes her weak and vulnerable to attack."

Sam nodded and folded her arms.

"Suit yourselves," said Gnanny. She shrugged and plopped down onto the floor.

The wooden floorboard creaked loudly. Gnipper cringed, expecting it to break under Gnanny's weight.

"So, where do I begin? You see children, there is this wonderful Dragon named Duncan the Magnificent. And like all old and powerful Dragons, he has abilities that we non-magical folk can hardly comprehend."

"What can we do?" Sam asked.

"He can see the future!" Gnanny smiled so wide, it looked like the moon—a bit yellow and full of craters.

"Wow," responded Gnipper. "That certainly would go against statistical probabilities." She twirled her hair while she ran the numbers in her head.

"You don't need to do the math," said Sam. "The Dragon is obviously lying."

Gnipper finished the calculation in her head anyway. There was less than a .00001 chance of that being true. Perhaps some type of ruse was in play. "Statistics agree with you."

Sam sighed. "You don't need statistics on this one, Gnip. You need logic. Think about it. If a creature with that kind of ability lived in Rosehaven, don't you think it would be known to everyone long before this? We don't exactly get a lot of new

Dragons in town. We've had the same group of seven since I was born, and none of them have ever been able to do anything even remotely magical. If we had a Dragon that could actually see the future, we wouldn't all need to be hiding on this island. We could return to our ancestral homes without fear of the Humans."

Gnipper nodded. Sam's logic was sound.

"Besides, Gnanny," Sam added. "How does this Dragon claiming to see the future have anything to do with you selling all your belongings?"

"I understand your disbelief completely, Sam. I suppose in your father's line of work he needs to be skeptical and question everything, and he has taught you to treat the world in the same manner, but I assure you I saw his power first hand. I sat directly across from him as he studied my eyes, and read the lines of my hands. Then, he told me my future—after years of not understanding or appreciating my creative talents, the citizens of Rosehaven undergo an epiphany—an understanding if you will. They'll demand an art show, which I will happily provide for them. And, at that highly successful exhibition, Duncan says I'll meet a very wealthy Gnome and fall madly in love. See, tell me that's not a perfect vision of the future."

"It is Gnanny," answered Sam. "It's too perfect."

"But," added Gnipper, "it's entirely possible. It's something that could happen."

"See Sam, Gnippy knows he has a real gift." Gnipper coughed as Gnanny wrapped her arms around her in a loving embrace.

"Sorry Gnanny, but Sam and I need to get going now."

"Already, you just arrived?"

"Uhhhh." Gnipper's eyes darted to the ceiling, as they did every time she was thinking of a lie. "Yes. We need to go because…because Sam has fleas. We just found out. She's itchy and needs a bath right away."

"Oh, poor girl, Gnanny said with a subtle step backwards. "Get her home right now and take care of that. Best way is to take a bath in fresh mint. Fleas hate it."

"Certainly, Gnanny. Mint bath, got it." Gnipper grabbed Sam by the arm and dragged her down the stairs and out the door.

"Fleas?" snapped Sam angrily. "Really? That's the best excuse you could come up with?"

"Sorry, I panicked."

"Tell me you don't really believe that this Dragon can see the future."

"No, you're right. It's statistically *and* logically impossible. Knowing the future would lead to the ability to change the future, therefore nullifying the initial knowledge in the first place. Besides, if he really had that power, Lord Laszlo would have him in the Council Chambers advising him, not living on the side of a mountain convincing people to pay him for snippets of their future. Gnanny likes what he had to say, so trying to convince her that her dream outcome is a lie is pointless. We need to show her he's lying."

"So what you're saying is—"

"We've got a downright devious Dragon to see today."

#

Gnipper couldn't believe the line. It meandered away from a raised platform, like a snake sunning itsElf on a rock. Waiting patiently were creatures of all shapes and sizes, species and races, colors and creeds. Yet, they all had one thing in common—they were all carrying large coin purses filled with golden Dragon-marks, small square coins that Rosehaven used as currency.

"Let's get in line," said Sam. "Hopefully, the wait isn't too long."

An hour passed before the girls had their turn come up. Gnipper was hot, and sweat drenched her, but she did her best to not complain about it. (Her best was not very good.)

The wait was made worse by two Ogres standing in front of them that blocked their view. They could hear though, as Duncan the Magnificent foretold prophecy after prophecy. Each of them promised riches, health, and happiness. No one questioned him, they just thanked him over and over again and poured their money into a wheelbarrow set up next to the stage. Gnipper led out a low growl of anger each time she heard the coins dropped in. These people were being taken advantage of, and she needed to put an end to it.

"You may approach," bellowed a deep, powerful voice. Finally, it was their turn. Gnipper got a bit nervous. She was barely over two feet tall, and here she was about to question the intentions of a giant Dragon that could roast her, bite her in half and swallow her. It seemed ludicrous, insane, even...

And that was when she finally saw him.

He was cobalt blue, shiny like a polished gem. His teeth were ivory razors waiting to clamp down on unsuspecting prey. His scales surrounded his body like impenetrable plates of armor. Oh, and he was barely the size of a fat house cat.

Gnipper chuckled as she passed his blond-maned Centaur bodyguard, and walked up the steps of the dais. "You're Duncan the Magnificent?" She struggled to keep the surprise out of her voice.

"The one and only. Seer of All Things Future. Knower of the Wonders of Tomorrow. Lord of That Which Has Not Yet Happened."

"I expected..." Gnipper stammered as she sat down across a wooden table from him.

"What? Bigger? That's pretty laughable coming from a Gnome. You above all should know that power is never limited by stature."

"I'm sorry," she answered. She truly was. She hated when people mocked her height, and she certainly didn't want to make another creature feel self-conscious.

"It's fine," he answered quickly. "Now how can I help you?"

He flashed her a friendly smile, but it made her feel even more apprehensive than she already was. She took a deep breath to calm herself before she spoke.

"We want you to give my Gnanny back her money that you stole."

The front of the line that was still waiting gasped. The back of the line followed suit in a delayed pattern as Gnipper's accusations were whispered along.

"Stole?!" He bellowed loud enough for everyone to hear. "How dare you accuse me of theft? I gave her a glimpse of her future, in exchange for a small fee. If anything, my information was so valuable, she robbed me."

A few murmurs of agreement went up from the crowd.

"You can't tell the future," snapped Gnipper. "It's statistically impossible to predict, due to the enormous amount of outcomes produced by every action and inaction we make every day."

"It's magic, my dear. Magic doesn't play by the rules."

"Magic doesn't beat science," she said confidently. "Ever." Gnipper stared him down, her nervousness faded. She'd seen magic before and it always adhered to rules and laws, just like science.

"Oh, it doesn't beat science, you say? I usually don't do this, but what if I gave you a brief sample, just to show you the extent of my talents?"

The crowd applauded. Gnipper wanted to turn around and yell at them. She was trying to help them not throw their life savings away and there they were cheering for the wrong team!

Gnipper looked at Sam for guidance. She nodded, letting her mane bounce in approval.

"Alright, fine," Gnipper said.

"Hold out your hand."

Gnipper put her hand out, palm up. The Dragon took it in his tiny claws, pressed his face up against it and examined each line on her skin. Everyone remained silent for several minutes, until finally he spoke.

"Yes. I see it now."

"You see what?" asked Gnipper.

"You are standing on a stage, in front of a large audience of Gnomes. It looks like the entire gnomish community is there. They are applauding. Now an older Gnome in a really tall white hat is putting one of those crazy Gnome caps on your head. You're smiling. Now everyone is chanting your name...Gnipper, Gnipper."

Gnipper reached her hand back. Excitement took her breath away. He had seen her receiving her pileus, the pointed hat that each member of the Gnomish community aspired to earn by inventing something for the good of society. Those who didn't earn their hat by their twelfth birthdays were labeled with the insult *gnit-wit*, an Old-Gnomish word meaning "one without adequate intelligence". Gnipper had been twelve for several months, and still hadn't earned hers. But now that was soon to change. The Dragon had seen it.

"I believe you," Gnipper said. She curtsied, the most respectful good-bye gesture she knew, turned and walked off the dais. The crowd gave Duncan a rousing ovation.

"What are you doing?" snapped Sam as she chased off the platform after her. Her fur was raised and her tail twitched.

"What? He's telling the truth. That's exactly how I expect the future will go." Gnipper couldn't get the image Duncan described out of her head. She'd dreamt of that moment since she was four days old. Excitement brimmed within her.

"Of course it is Gnip, he told you exactly what you want to hear."

Sam was annoyed. She just didn't understand. Duncan couldn't be wrong. He just knew too much. "Sam, I know it seems that way, but how else would he know that I'm trying to earn my hat."

"You're a Gnome with a frying pan on you your head."

"It's a skillet."

Sam raised one eyebrow and stared down at her.

"But he knew my name," Gnipper continued. "And who my dad is."

"He's met Gnanny. She probably told him everything he needed to know to trick you. He's a con artist, that's what he does."

Gnipper dropped her gaze to the floor. Sam was right. She wanted that to be her future, so she let Duncan convince her. It was exactly the reason Gnanny and all the others believed him—because they wanted to. She knew it going in, and he was still able to fool her.

"What do we do about it, Sam? If he's telling everyone what they want to hear, how are we going to convince them he's lying? I couldn't even figure out how to convince my own Gnanny, let alone the entire town."

"Maybe this isn't something we should be doing. I think we need to talk to the Sheriff."

#

Gnipper had been to the Sheriff's office once before. One of her neighbors had claimed she tried to kill them and burn their house down. She calmly explained that she was just testing her new high powered, steam operated water hose, and that their house was more flammable than hers, so it made a better testing facility. It would have been perfect, if she had remembered to put the other end of the hose in the well. Those neighbors never did rebuild their house.

It was just like she remembered it—a small wooden building, with three desks, and two metal barred cells in the back. It wasn't fancy, and neither was the Sheriff—Kirgo Quicktrigger.

He was an older Dwarf with bushy white hair and a neatly braided matching beard. He had a chubby, friendly face and wore a loose fitting leather vest over a white cotton shirt. At his side he carried an old flintlock pistol with an ornately engraved ivory handle. Gnipper's father had made it for him many years before, with some "unique" modifications.

Everyone in Rosehaven loved him. Well, everyone who obeyed the law loved him. Everyone else just tried their best to avoid him.

"What can I do for you, young ladies?" He asked.

"We'd like to report a crime, Sheriff. Duncan the Dragon is pretending he can see the future and taking everyone's Dragon-marks."

"Yeah," he said as he sat back in his chair and ran his hand down his beard. "I've heard about that."

"You have?" Sam asked. "How come you haven't arrested him?"

"Cause he's not breaking the law."

"But he's lying," Gnipper added. Gnipper was sure there had to be something illegal about lying.

"I agree, but there's no way to prove it. He doesn't ever tell anyone when these things are going to happen, so there's not a way to prove that they won't. Without a confession, there's nothing I can do."

"So, he can just swindle people? Destroy their lives?" Gnipper felt her face getting hot. She was annoyed.

The Sheriff slowly shook his head. "Unless you have a way to get him to tell the truth on his own, I'm afraid so."

Gnipper smiled and sat up straight in her chair. It was a crooked smile, the type that plastered itself to her face whenever she had one of her great ideas.

"Sam," she said excitedly, "I need to get back to my lab."

******

Sam strode through market square with a quick, determined gait. Gnipper wouldn't tell her the plan after they left the Sheriff's office the day before, and that made her nervous. The little Gnome had just said "trust me" and scampered off to her lab. That was never a good sign.

"I can't buy this fruit. You charge too much and it looks bruised."

Sam stopped to listen to an Elf complain to Elmira Applebottom, a homely Dryad with a screechy voice, but one of the best fruit vendors on the island. The Elf seemed annoyed.

"I didn't want to sell it to you anyway," Elmira answered. "You smell funny and it makes my nostrils burn."

"You're ugly, and the rest of the dryads find you annoying. They tell everyone."

Elmira grabbed the Elf's long blond hair, let out a short scream and began yanking as hard as she could. Sam turned to intercede in the fight, but several other patrons had already begun to break them up.

"What was that about?" thought Sam as she continued along. Elmira was the last person in Rosehaven that would be in a fight. Dryads were creatures of the forest, and known for being peaceful and passive.

Her thoughts were interrupted by a young lime-skinned Goblin. His pointed nose dripped snot, and his face was covered in oozing acne. Dire-lice (like regular lice, but three times as big) danced through his hair like they were acrobats and his scalp was their stage. He smelled of rotting garbage, and his clothes were barely good enough to be rags, let alone body coverings.

"Excuse me, Miss?" asked the Goblin.

He was holding a dusty Dragon-mark, not a huge sum of money but enough for a good lunch and some new clothes.

"Someone must have dropped it. I want to keep it. I really want to keep it. But for some reason, I need to find the rightful owner."

"Sorry, I've never seen it before." The Goblin looked both relieved, and annoyed at the same time.

"I guess I'll keep looking, while secretly hoping I never find the owner."

"Good luck with that," answered Sam. Weird, thought Sam, everyone seems to be...telling the truth.

Sam hissed through clenched teeth. She wasn't sure how Gnipper did it, but she was sure she did it. And now, like always, she was going to have to spend her day helping Gnipper clean up the mess.

Gnipper was cleaning up the lab when Sam barged in.

"What did you do?" Sam asked. She said each word slowly and drawn out, so that Gnipper would know she was serious.

"I merely solved our little Dragon problem," Gnipper answered as she continued to clean.

"The entire town is being truthful. It's making them fight!"

"Not the entire town. Only the ones who have indoor plumbing or get their water from the central well."

"You poisoned the well?!"

"Noooo, not poisoned. Serumed. Truth serum to be exact. My own blend. Not only does it make it impossible for a person to tell a lie, but it gives them an uncontrollable urge to reveal information they would normally keep inside."

"Gnipper, why would you put it in the well? There was practically a brawl at the Market from this stuff! Elmira Applebottom nearly ripped an Elf's hair out of her head."

"Hmmmm…" said Gnipper as she slowly twirled one of the wilder sections of her rose-pink hair. "Unfortunate side effect, but it couldn't be avoided."

"Making everyone in town angry and upset is an unfortunate side effect?"

"The truth hurts, Sam. But don't fret, it should wear off before sundown."

"Hopefully, Rosehaven doesn't have any riots before then. So what happens now?"

"Now, my furry friend, we go talk to a truthful little blue Dragon."

****

The line in front of Duncan's was even longer than the day before, and a whole lot angrier. Dwarves told each other what they really thought about each other's beard-dos, faeries gave each other unwanted criticism on how well their make-up matched their wings, and elves...well the elves seemed about the same as always.

Gnipper peered up and down the line, seeing the squabbles, hurt feelings, and random punches. Perhaps she had been a bit hasty putting the truth serum in the well. If she had put her gigantic gnomish brain to the task, she was sure she could have found a better way. She really had to learn to stop rushing into things.

"Alright Gnip, here's the plan. I'll call him out on his lies and you keep track of everything he says for the Sheriff. You're sure the serum works on a Dragon, right?"

"Without a doubt! There is absolutely no reason this plan shouldn't work."

Sam stepped forward to the front of the crowd.

"Duncan," shouted Sam above the noisy arguments of the crowd. "The citizens of Rosehaven demand you answer our questions."

Everyone stopped bickering and turned their attention to Sam.

"I never demanded anything," whispered a voice from the line.

"She's very loud," said another.

"She needs to learn manners and she smells like acorns," announced a third.

Gnipper nodded. Truth serum in the town well was definitely not her best move.

"Who summons the great and almighty Duncan from his Sanctuary of Seeing?"

"I did, Duncan. And it's a three foot raised platform with a table, not a 'sanctuary of seeing.'"

He gave a sharp toothed grin. "Back again, little Squirrelkin? I don't think I caught your name yesterday."

"Samantha Alain Bushytail, daughter of Alastar Bushytail, Captain of the Acorn guard."

Gnipper's eyes opened wide. Sam never used her middle name. It had been her mother's.

"And you brought Gnipper back with you as well, I see."

Gnipper waved in a slow side to side motion like she was in a parade. She could feel her cheeks begin to turn the same shade of pink as her hair, as she felt the annoyed eyes of Duncan's line of "customers" peering at her. She hoped Sam got to the point quick.

"Duncan, we come with only one question. Can you really see you future?"

The crowd moved their gaze back to Duncan, awaiting his answer.

Gnipper smiled. Now they would all see just what a gigantic fraud he really was. Gnanny and the rest of the people of Rosehaven could demand their stuff be returned, and everyone could go back to enjoying another beautiful day on the island.

"Fine folks of Rosehaven, a question has been posed, and as I see blunt and brutal honesty is the code of the day, I too must confess something."

The crowd got eerily silent, waiting for Duncan to finish.

Gnipper's hands shook in anticipation. This was it. He'd tell the truth, and everyone would be so happy that the Board of Knowledgeable Gnomes would have to give her a *pileus* for her amazing work with truth serum.

"I must confess," he continued after a pause, "that I cannot see the future."

Got him!

"No," he continued. "To simply see the future isn't right. I experience the future. I see the events, I hear the sounds, and smell the odors. I feel it all. The future is mine!"

The crowd broke into riotous applause.

Gnipper was stunned. It didn't work. Why didn't the serum work? Ninety-four percent of the citizens of Rosehaven had indoor plumbing supplied by that well (thanks to Gnomes of course). The rest, like Sam, lived outside the city limits in the forest. The chance that he wouldn't have gotten water from the well was very small.

"While often a blessing," Duncan added, "as I get to know things that will keep you, my fellow citizens, out of trouble, my gift is also a curse. It's a curse when it brings out the lack of trust and sheer ignorance of our youth. But I suppose that ignorance is why one would be a gnit-wit anyway."

The crowd broke into uncontrolled laughter. Gnipper's heart sank. She had been insulted with that word many times by her father, and the other Gnomes, but never by so many who didn't even know her. Her face began to burn with rage, and tears welled with hurt. She opened her mouth to scream back at him, to hurt him the way he hurt her, but Sam had already grabbed her shoulder and spun her around.

She took one last glance back and watched Duncan open a jug of water. He pointed at it, smiled, and took a sip.

Gnipper's jaw dropped. He had known about the well, and had a private stock of water! He had been one step ahead of them the entire time. He had outsmarted her.

Sam didn't speak the entire time they walked back to the lab. The silence made Gnipper feel worse. She wished Sam would just lash out at her. Tell her how she messed everything up and how she was a failure. Finally, as they arrived back and Gnipper was surrounded by beakers, flasks, and chemicals- all the things that made her comfortable in life—Gnipper decided to speak first.

"I'm sorry, Sam. I really thought the truth serum would work."

"Sorry? For what? For doing your best to help your family and your community? For standing up against evil? For trying something most would only dream about? Sure the well idea had a few minor hiccups, but nothing that won't be over in a few hours. So tell me Gnipper, what exactly are you sorry for?"

"For being a failure." Gnipper dropped her head and stared at the floor. She didn't want Sam to see the tears in her eyes.

"Failure? Oh, so you're giving up?"

"No. I just--"

"You said you were a failure. Well, one thing my father always taught me was that failure is an outcome, and you can't achieve an outcome until the very end."

"What do you mean?"

"I mean that the only way you're a failure is if you give up and stop trying. As long as you never give up and keep working until you get the outcome you want, then it's simply not possible to be a failure. Think of it like an experiment. Is an experiment a failure when it's only halfway through?"

Gnipper perked up. Sam was right. Gnanny still needed her. Rosehaven needed her. This wasn't over yet! She just needed a new idea.

"Come back early tomorrow, Sam. We've got a Dragon to outsmart."

Sam smiled at her, gave her a quick hug, and darted up the stairs.

She was glad Sam wasn't mad at her, because the Squirrel-kin was absolutely going to hate her new plan.

******

Sam was there bright and early the next day, just as Gnipper had asked.

"So what's the plan, Gnipper?"

"Well, the truth serum works. We know that much."

"No doubt about that. My father spent three hours last night telling me about all the citizens of Rosehaven that he doesn't trust. It was not a fun conversation. It actually wasn't a conversation at all…it was more of a list."

"We also know that Duncan knows about the serum, and has planned for it. He also knows our faces and won't let us anywhere near him again."

"Yeah, he's smart. He'll be expecting us."

"So we need a face he's never seen before. Or perhaps several faces."

"You don't mean…"

"I've asked Bartlebee to help us."

"Your old lab Brownie? Gnipper that's crazy. He doesn't even remember who he is since the accident."

Sam was right. It had been over a year since Bartlebee was…well Bartlebee. It all started one afternoon when he had been cleaning up the lab. A rather impressively powered sneeze sent him reeling into a vat of what Gnipper called "let's-see-what-happens-sauce". She had fished him out after only a few seconds, but the damage had been done. Ever since he had been...very different.

"Not sure who this Brownie is that you speak of, but If I might be obliged to offer my services."

Gnipper looked over to the tiny creature on her lab table. Bartlebee was about four inches tall. He had a short blond beard on his chin, and was dressed all in forest green, including tights, a pointed woodsman cap with a red feather, and a simple cloth tunic. He carried a bow and had an arrow filled quiver on his back.

"You see, young Gnipper here had expressed to me this dastardly conundrum you face. It is truly a wicked tale of deceit and loss, but a tale I've heard before. More importantly it's a tale I've lived before- the wicked overlord stealing from the coffers of the downtrodden. You're story merely needs a dashing hero to set right the wrongs of this dastardly interloper. I, young maidens fair, shall be that hero."

Sam looked at him quizzically before whispering into Gnipper's ear.

"Who is he today?"

"Robin of Locksley. Better known to the world as Robin Hood."

"Robin Hood? He thinks he's a bird with a head covering?"

"Really, Sam? Didn't your father ever read any Human books to you?"

"No. He says the only stories worth hearing are the ones you make yourself."

"Well, Robin Hood is a Human legend. He's a nobleman turned outlaw that led a rebellion against an evil Sheriff. The Sheriff had been using taxes to steal money from the people and Robin Hood stood up to him."

"So he lied and stole, just like Duncan is doing."

"And now we've got a miniature version of Robin Hood to stand up to him."

"How is that going to help us?"

"Don't worry Sam. I've got a plan. We just need disguises."

It was busier than ever when they arrived, and blending into the crowd was easy with their traveling cloaks pulled up around their heads. No one gave them a second look as they drifted towards the front of the line. Sam took Bartlebee out from under her lavender cloak and placed him on the floor.

"Who's next?" asked Duncan's bodyguard. Several members of the crowd raised their hands, but Bartlebee was too quick for them. He had already bounded up onto the dais, climbed a chair to the table, and stood in front of Duncan's face.

"I, Robin of Locksley, am next foul Dragon."

"Robin of what now?" asked Duncan.

"You might know me as Robin Hood."

"Nope, never head of you, but I assume you've brought payment?"

"I've brought coin, you knave, but I attest I won't be as easy to swindle as these good trusting folk."

"Oh another one that questions my abilities? Why don't you let me get a quick look at your hand, and I can tell you all about your future, then we'll see who the true nave is."

Bartle-hood held his bow in one hand and reached his other hand out. Duncan took it delicately between two talons and began to examine it closely.

"It looks here that you are an archer?"

"The greatest in all the land."

"I see that. In the future it appears that you are going to win an important archery contest."

"Undoubtedly," answered Bartle-hood.

"Gnipper," whispered Sam, "He seems to be telling him the right things. When does your plan start to work?"

"Just listen. Trust me."

"And I bet you do well with the ladies."

"Of course," Bartle-hood said with a chuckle, "but there's just one maiden for my heart."

"Yes. I see you two getting married and having many children together."

"Beautiful little treasures I'm sure."

"Yes, truly adorable little tykes. And the best part, you and your maiden-together you will become rich and powerful and rule the land as King!"

"There it is," announced Gnipper.

Bartlebee-Robin's face turned to a scowl as he drew his hand back.

"You dare to mock me?"

"Mock you, what are you talking about? Don't you want to be rich?"

"Long ago did I cast off the blanket of privilege and nobility to fight for the rights of the poor, yet you have the audacity to call me a traitor to my own beliefs? Not only that, but you believe that I would usurp the crown from the rightful head of my Lord, King Richard the Lionhearted?"

"What are you talking about?" Duncan asked, the confusion plastered to his leathery face. "It's in the future. You can't argue with the future."

"Not for me, it's not. I've already lived this life and a dozen more. At no point in my tenure upon this earth will Robin of Loxley become a slave to gold and power. I live and die by the outlaw's code, protecting the people from the tyranny you claim I become. With this insult, I challenge you to a duel!"

"What? You're barely the size of my little talon. I would—"

As Duncan spoke a tiny arrow hit him square in the eye. It wasn't enough to pierce through, or harm him in any permanent way. But, judging by the way he screamed, it was enough to hurt him.

Duncan's centaur bodyguard made a quick grab for Bartlehood, but the Brownie was too quick, he jumped back, loosing another arrow. This one hit the bodyguard in his ear, piercing through and sticking out like a piece of jewelry.

"Owwwwww," he screamed as he dropped to the floor with a loud thud, clutching the side of his head.

"Remind me not to hire him," laughed Gnipper as she watched the bodyguard slink off the platform and away from the Brownie.

"I'm gonna kill you," snapped Duncan as he pounced back up onto the table. His left eye was swelled shut, but Dragon's had other tools. He opened his mouth, and let out a small burst of flame.

He ducked, as the flame engrossed his entire body.

The crowd gasped as they watched the Brownie become incinerated in front of their very eyes.

As the flame stopped, and the smoke cleared. Bartlehood stood, uninjured except for some singed hair.

"How did he—" asked Sam.

"Fireproof clothing," Gnipper answered. "I invented it last night. Completely protects the wearer from temperatures up to 3,000 degrees Gnomenheit."

Duncan was stunned—his jaw dropped and he took a few small steps back.

Bartle-hood took the opportunity to press his attack. Another arrow launched, poking Duncan in his other eye.

"Oh no, I'm blind." (He wasn't. the arrows barely poked him. He'd be fine in ten minutes)

"What Dragon? Didn't you see that in your own future? No? Perhaps it's because you're nothing more than a fraud! Admit it now, in front of all these people."

"Nonsense," Duncan cried. "It's just that my gift doesn't work that way."

"Perhaps you just need some motivation to tell the truth."

Bartle-hood dropped his bow and pulled his long sword. (Which was actually Professor Tallhat's favorite letter opener.) He darted toward Duncan, swiping quickly at the Dragon's arms and face and giving him dozens of paper cut sized wounds.

Duncan swiped back, but without vision or use of fire, Bartle-hood just danced out of the way of his blows, and swiped back with his "sword".

"Oh stop," Duncan screamed after a particularly deep cut to his nostril. "Fine, I'll tell the truth. I can't see the future. I was making it all up. I was just telling people what they wanted to hear."

The crowd gasped. Dozens screamed for their money back. Other's screamed for Duncan so that they could do the kind of things to him that mobs liked to do to people they were angry at.

Boom.

A gunshot rang out behind Gnipper's head. She jumped, startled by the abrupt sound.

The crowd got silent as everyone waited to see what was happening. The anger had made them brave enough to keep from running, but not brave enough to keep yelling and drawing attention to themselves.

From just behind Gnipper a barrel-chested Dwarf pushed past, dropping his hood off his head.

"Sheriff Quicktrigger?" said Sam.

"Drop the letter opener, Bartlebee."

The Sheriff strode onto the platform and grabbed Duncan by his wings.

"Duncan Silverclaw, you are under arrest for fraud, theft, and attempted murder."

"What? No! It's the crazy Brownie. Not me. He attacked me. Aren't you going to arrest him?"

"Arrest my deputy? I don't think so."

"Arrest your what?"

"A little pink-haired Gnome came to me yesterday with an interesting plan to end an ongoing crime. It just required that I deputize Bartlebee here and put him undercover. Any actions he took today were done for the protection of Rosehaven. As for you, you're gonna have a lot of time to think about what you did to these nice people. Let's go."

The sheriff picked him up by his neck (to make sure he couldn't breathe fire again) and carried him off toward The Pit, Rosehaven's underground prison.

"Gnipper," said Sam excitedly. "You did it. You outsmarted Duncan."

"Eh, Bartlebee did most of the work. I just figured if we presented Duncan with a Human, who went against the Human nature toward greed, that he'd never be able to predict the outcome. Since Bartlebee already knew everything about Robin Hood, he would know that Duncan was lying, and of course thinking he was a famous outlaw, he would want to duel. Then, all I had to do was make sure he didn't commit any crimes and that the Sheriff was here to see it all. Honestly, it was nothing. Now the fire-proof clothing--that I'm proud of."

"Uh, Gnipper."

"Seriously, I can't wait to submit that to the Board of Knowledgeable Gnomes for consideration. There's no chance that won't earn me my pileus. That hat's going to be mine Sam, finally."

"Uh, Gnip."

"Sam I'm trying to plan my acceptance speech for my hat. Why do you keep interrupting?"

"Look behind you."

Gnipper turned. Bartle-hood had been bowing and playing to the crowd, when suddenly his green clothing began to disintegrate.

He was too busy bowing to notice he was now naked, on the stage, and that people were running and covering their eyes."

"Okay, so maybe that one still needs a bit of work."

"It's okay Gnip. You'll get it right. Remember, failure is an outcome, and you can't have an outcome until the end."

"And the end can't come if you don't ever give up."

Sam smiled and put her arm around Gnipper. Gnipper smiled back.

She might not have earned her hat today, but tomorrow was a new day with new ideas.

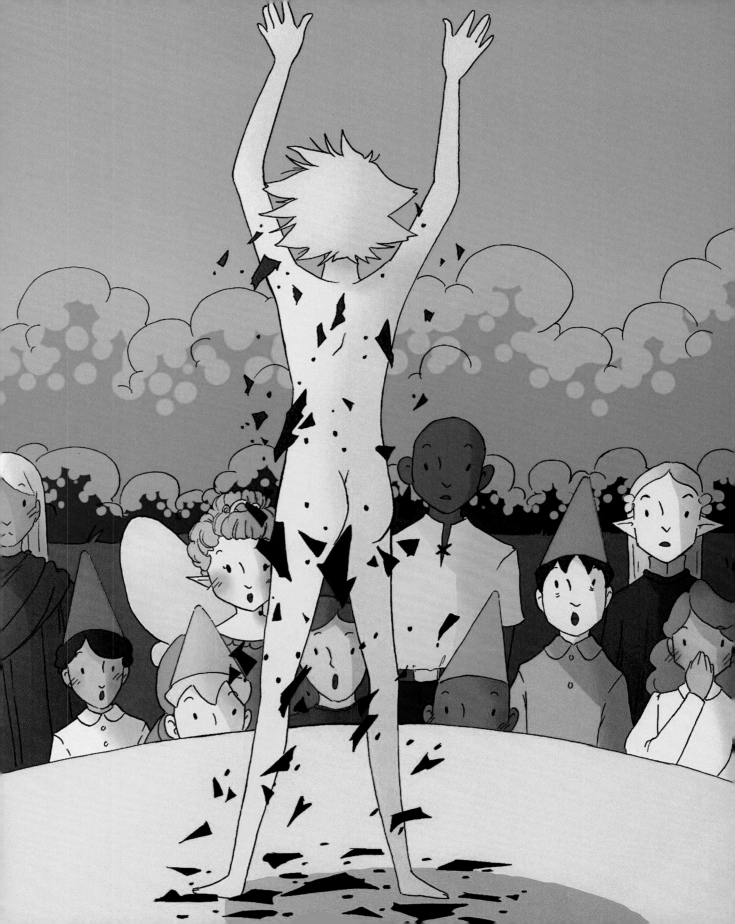

Want More Rosehaven? Check out these fine stories:

Rise of the Retics (Rosehaven Book 1)
Return of the Fae-blood (Rosehaven Book 2)

Gnit-Wit Gnipper and the Perilous Plague
Gnit-Wit Gnipper and the Ferocious Fire-Ants
Gnit-Wit Gnipper and the Devious Dragon

Sir Dudley Tinklebutton and the Dragon's Lair
Sir Dudley Tinklebutton and the Sword of Cowardice
Sir Dudley Tinklebutton and the Unholy Grail

Sign up for T.J.'s Monthly Newsletter here

Or follow him on Facebook

T.J. Lantz is from York, Pa where he was an elementary school teacher. He currently lives in the Caribbean nation of Grenada with his wife Maya, who is studying to be a Veterinarian, his daughters Arya and Piper, and his three dogs. He enjoys dreaming about the day he gets to return to America and escape the giant island insects that want to kill him.

Ana Santo is a freelance illustrator who has recently left the science field to follow her dream of being an artist. She is currently working on multiple graphic novel projects.

56343768R00031

Made in the USA
Middletown, DE
13 December 2017